The Race of 12 Zodiac

First Published in Australia in 2020 by A Mythical Story Pty Limited.
4/105a Vanessa Street Kingsgrove NSW Australia 2208
Visit our website at www.amythicalstory.com

A Mythical Story Pty Limited.

Title: The Race of 12 Zodiac
ISBN: 9780645068412
Series: A Mythical Story - A Chinese Mythical Story
Target Audience: For Children
Distribution: Amazon-Kindle Direct Publishing

Cover & internal design: Bubupandaaa

Acknowledgements:

Dedicated to Australian Yau Kung Mun members for their support and dedication to the art of Lion Dance over the years, with special thanks to JuJu Man, Stefan Desmid and Andrew Lau for their contributions to the story.

©

The Jade Emperor held a race that the first 12 animals will determine the order of time.

On race day, all the animals gathered at the starting line.

The smartest of them all, the Rat asked the gentle Ox for help to cross the river.

The Sheep, the Monkey and the Rooster decided to team up.

Whilst the Dog and the Pig were just interested in playing.

The Tiger jumped into the river without thinking, but the strong current made it tough to paddle across.

The Rabbit decided to find another way, jumping from rock to rock and crossed the river.

The Dragon has a heart of gold, and helped a young boy retrieve a pearl from the top of a mountain.

The Snake can swim and slithered across the river.

The Horse marched proudly putting one foot infront of the other.

As the Ox crosses the river and reached the other side, the Rat leapt forward and won the race.

The Ox came second.

After a battle with the waves, the Tiger reached the other side and crossed the finish line.

The rabbit arrived forth.

As the Horse approached the end, the Snake slithered infront and startled him.

So the Snake came sixth and the Horse came seventh.

The Sheep, the Monkey and the Rooster built a raft and drifted across the river to come in eighth, ninth and tenth.

After playing in the water, the Dog paddled his way to the finish line coming eleventh.

Finally the Pig, who was distracted by food, came in last.

Each zodiac animal represents your personality, each with different strengths and characteristics.

What Zodiac animal are you?